Gardenias and Oranges

Jo Ann Yolanda Hernández

SCHOLASTIC INC.
New York Toronto London Auckland Sydney
Mexico City New Delhi Hong Kong

**Cover and interior illustrations by
Laura Jacobsen**

Copyright © 2001 by Scholastic Inc.
All rights reserved. Published by Scholastic Inc.
Printed in the U.S.A.

ISBN 0-439-31278-7

SCHOLASTIC, READ 180, and associated logos and designs are
trademarks and/or registered trademarks of Scholastic Inc.
LEXILE is a trademark of MetaMetrics, Inc.

5   6   7   8   9   10   23   10 09 08 07 06 05

Contents

Watch That Watch

The moment I dreaded was coming down on me fast. I couldn't make dinner last forever, but I tried. I kept eating and eating. Only my girlfriend, Amelia, and her mother remained at the table with me.

At first, Mrs. Ramirez raised her eyebrows. Then she shrugged her shoulders and loaded more food on my plate. It wasn't long before I was on my third helping. By then the grin on Mrs. Ramirez' face was so wide, my mouth ached just to look at it.

Sad to say, Mrs. Ramirez was not the best cook in the world, so she was not used to people asking for extra servings. Amelia figured I was just trying to be nice to her mother. Silently, her

lips formed the words, "Thank you." I stabbed a clump of stuffing with my fork and shoveled it in. If Amelia only knew the real reason why I was acting this way, she'd kick me to the curb faster than you could say "trash day."

When she took my empty plate, I jumped up to help Mrs. Ramirez clear the dishes. Again, Mrs. Ramirez looked at me with question marks in her eyes. She elbowed Amelia and called me a very considerate young man. Amelia looked at me and said, "Hilario, don't worry about it. Go keep my father company." She gave my arm a squeeze. She was so proud of me. I felt lower than a worm.

In the living room, Amelia's two younger brothers played on the floor with their new remote-controlled cars. It had been a good Christmas for the Ramirez family. Amelia's father watched the game on his new big-screen TV. He said something about the Cowboys winning.

It was hard for me to pay attention to the game. I kept wondering how much longer it would be until I had to face Amelia alone.

Finally, Amelia and Mrs. Ramirez came out of the kitchen. I rose from my chair. I had to think of something fast, so I thanked Amelia's mother again for dinner. She cracked another big smile. Then I said I had to leave. It was lame, but that was all I could think of.

Amelia tilted her head a little to the side. "Already?" She looked hurt.

At the door, she said, "Wait there just a minute, Hilario."

"Amelia…"

But it was too late; she had already run off to her bedroom. In a flash she was back with my Christmas present. What could I do? I unwrapped the silver paper and flipped open the plastic box. A gold watch glinted at me. I stumbled over my words. "Uh, this is really nice, Amelia."

"Something special for someone special." She leaned against the front door with her hand on the doorknob. Amelia's parents were strict. They counted the minutes we stood there.

I hung my head and scraped the floor with my foot. I hoped the right words would come

into my head and out of my mouth in the right way. Instead, I heard myself mumble, "I sort of left your present at home. I'll bring it tomorrow when we take your brothers to the video arcade."

"Listen," I said. "It's just a little thing. It's nothing like what you gave me."

"It's from you," Amelia said, looking into my eyes. "That's all that matters. Right?"

I scraped my foot again. "Yeah, I guess so."

What's bothering Hilario? Why do you think he's acting this way?

2 Orange Crush

The next morning, with the Texas sun bright, I called my cousin. "Armando, you got to help me out."

Armando raced across the backyards of the few houses between our homes. He sat next to me on the back porch.

Before he reached the steps, I said, "I've got big-time trouble."

"Whatever," Armando said with a grin. "We stick together."

I shook my head. "See this?" I held up my wrist.

"Amelia gave you that watch?"

I nodded.

"What did you give her?"

"I told her I forgot her present at home."

"So?"

"I freaked when I saw what she gave me. I had to say something." I searched my cousin's eyes for the answer to my love problem.

Armando, his eyes the dark of a midnight sky, said, "You didn't tell her about…"

"Nah. "

Armando nodded.

"Got any money left?"

We dug in our pockets.

Armando picked out the junk. I counted the coins.

"$1.13, cuz," I said.

"Not good, *primo*."

"Amelia's never going to forgive me." I flopped onto the wooden steps and leaned back on my elbows. "She's my *reyna*. What will I do without my queen?"

We stared out into the sun-bright colors of the garden, but the flowers did nothing to stop the worry warping my mind.

Armando chewed on a toothpick. "Hey, I got it, man."

I glanced up.

"She's a *chavala*." He waved the toothpick in the air.

"Yes, I know she's a girl." I stared at him.

primo	=	cousin
reyna	=	queen
chavala	=	girl

"They're all tender-hearted. Just put something together. She'll think you're sweet."

"Put something together? Like what?"

The toothpick snapped in his hand. "I don't know, man. Something . . . like a bunch of flowers." He tossed the splintered toothpick over his shoulder.

I hopped up. "I know." I checked for my mother through the screen door, then crept through her garden and broke off three huge gardenias.

Armando grinned.

I strutted by him into the kitchen. I came out a few minutes later, twisting a rubber band around the stems of the three gardenias. "Now what?" I stood on the top step.

Armando looked at me, studied the gardenias in my hand, then leaped up. "I got an idea. Get a bag. Hurry up." He dashed around the house.

I raced back into the kitchen, hid the gardenias behind the trash can, grabbed a brown paper bag and trailed after my cousin.

Armando stopped at the edge of the

corner house, standing next to the white picket fence. "Here."

I saw nothing but the cars going by and kids playing across the street. "I've got no time for your jokes."

Armando thumped his chest with his thumb. "Man, you're thick. Amelia should be in love with me."

"Hey, watch it."

Armando pointed. "The tree. Pick her some oranges."

"Oranges? Are you crazy or what?"

"No, *primo*. She'll think you went out of your way for her."

"I don't know. Sounds pretty stupid."

"You rather show up with nothing and see her get all sad?" Armando grinned. "And she'll probably cry."

I placed one foot on the picket fence. Armando gave me a boost. I grabbed the lowest branch and swung my legs onto the tree. I picked a few oranges and tossed them to Armando, who caught them like baseballs and dumped them into the bag. He stretched

out his T-shirt like a basket to catch one more.

Then we heard barking. From a flap in the front door, a black spot appeared. The one spot multiplied into two spots. The spots became dogs rushing to get at us. I released the oranges I held in my arms. They showered over Armando.

He rubbed his head. "Hey, that hurt!"

The first Doberman reached the fence and lunged at the tree. I leaped down, knocking Armando over when I hit the ground. The dogs snarled and jumped. They were trying to jump the fence!

Armando shoved me off him. I fell backwards landing with an "oof!" I felt my backside go wet as the orange I landed on turned into orange mush.

The dogs sounded like fifty dogs rather than two hungry ones. They looked like they were sizing us up for lunch.

"C'mon, cuz. Let's get out of here," I said.

Armando scrambled up and pitched an orange at the dogs. It splattered yellow against the white fence. I snatched up the paper bag and ran after my cousin. The growling dogs, with their ears piercing the sky, ran alongside us on the other side of the fence.

We could still hear the dogs howling when we rounded the corner of our block. Old Man Gonzales had said we could pick some of his oranges—too bad no one told his dogs.

I cleaned up, changed my clothes, and sat next to Armando on the back steps. He sniffed at me.

"Okay, cousin. I got the gardenias, and I got the oranges. Now what?" I asked him.

"You've got to write Amelia something romantic." Armando puckered and made kissing noises.

"Romantic? I don't know how to write romantic junk."

"Doesn't matter. Write whatever. Girls get all teary-eyed over any little thing." Armando shoved me. "Just tell her the truth."

"You're crazy, cousin."

My mother stuck her head out from around the screen door. "Hilario, Amelia's on the phone for you."

I got up.

Armando tripped me and laughed.

I dragged my feet toward the house and answered the phone. "Hey."

"Hilario, when are you gonna get here?"

"I told you I would be there."

"My brothers are pestering me to go to the arcade. And I was hoping you would bring my present soon."

"Listen, I told you. It's hardly anything at all."

"That doesn't matter, honey. If it comes from your heart, that's all that counts."

I hung up. Outside, I flopped down next to Armando. "Her brothers want to go to the arcade already."

"She's gonna bury you alive," Armando laughed.

"What kind of friend are you?"

"I figured out the flowers and the oranges already for you. I told you to write the note, man. What else you want me to do? Write the note for you?"

"Nah, I can do that."

"Just tell her the truth. Girls dig that kind of stuff."

"I just don't know," I mumbled.

Armando left to run an errand for his mother with a promise to come back once he was done.

Do you think Amelia will like Hilario's gift? Why or why not?

3

Dear Amelia . . .

In my bedroom, at my desk, I pulled out my notebook and tore out a clean page. I held the pen in my hand and wrote "Dear Amelia," across the top of the sheet. Next I wrote, "I want to tell you . . . ," and then my pen ran out of ink.

I threw the pen away and found a pencil. I stared at a new page, but my hand wouldn't move. My mind was as blank as the lines on the page. I knew I'd never be able to fill the whole page with words.

I kept trying to write something. I erased so many times I dug a hole through the paper. Then I started a new page, then another and another. I couldn't think of anything to say, so I wrote the truth.

Armando knocked on the door as he walked in. "Did you write the letter?"

"I did." I licked the envelope closed.

"Let me read it."

"You crazy? No way." I held the envelope away from his outstretched hand.

"Why not?" He eyed me with a cocked eyebrow. "You told her the truth?"

"Yeah, I told her what happened. I just know she's gonna hate me forever."

"No, cousin, you'll see. It's all gonna work out." He stood up. "Let's go."

"What you mean, 'Let's go'?" I put on my jacket, sticking the letter in the pocket. "I'm going by myself. I don't want you messing things up." I picked up the bag of oranges, snatched up the gardenias, and headed out.

What do you think Hilario's letter says?

4 Time's Up

Armando tracked me down the hallway and out of the house. "I'm the one that came up with the plan. Anyway, you'll need help with her brothers if you want to get all mushy-mushy with Amelia."

"Get out of my face."

He kept after me, saying, "This is how you show your gratitude when someone sticks by you, even in the jaws of man-eating dogs?"

I rounded the corner of Amelia's block. "There wouldn't have been any man-eating dogs if you hadn't dragged me out there." I stopped at the sight of Amelia's house. "Armando, stay here. I've got to do this alone."

"You just don't want anyone around when she tells you to get lost."

My mouth fell open. "I thought you said this plan would work."

Armando shrugged. "Who knows with *chavalas*?"

I turned away rather than slug him and went to the front door. Amelia opened the door before I knocked. Her brothers ran by us and raced to Armando and jumped on his back. They wrestled on the grass.

Amelia's smile made my heart feel good, but sad, too. This might be the last time she'd smile like that for me.

She stepped out onto the porch and hugged me tight. "Oh, you smell good. Like oranges. Did you get a new cologne?"

I shook my head. She waited.

I stuck out my hands with the three drooping gardenias. "I told you I didn't have much."

She oohed and took them. Sticking them under her nose, Amelia said, "They're so beautiful."

This fed my courage a little, so I pushed the paper bag between us. "This, too."

Amelia peeked inside the bag. "Oranges. My favorite. Oh, Hilario, you're so sweet."

Before I could scare myself out of doing it, I handed her the envelope. "This is for you, too. Let's get to the arcade before your brothers beat up Armando." I turned to go down the front steps.

She pulled me back with her hand on my arm. "No, wait. Let me read the letter first."

I stood, staring at my new Christmas sneakers while she read the letter. Armando stood behind the neighbor's tree, blocking her bratty brothers from coming over and bothering us.

She stopped reading and glanced sideways at me. She had tears in her eyes.

"I'm sorry, Amelia."

"Hilario, you're so, so…" She flung her arms around my neck. Her tears wet my cheeks. "Your mother already told me. When her sewing machine broke, you gave her all your money so she could finish the holiday dress for your little sister. You're the most generous guy I've ever known."

I hugged Amelia. My arms felt nice around her. We stayed like that for a minute.

Then Armando started laughing at me from behind the tree. As he stuck his thumb in the air, I guessed he was telling Amelia's brothers, "Girls go for dumb stuff like the truth."

Why do you think it took Hilario so long to tell Amelia the truth?

Meet the Author

I didn't always know that I was going to be a writer. But I always liked to write. In high school, I wrote a 25-page ending to a story and got an "F" because I misspelled so many words. I was 33 when I took my first writing class in college and realized that I had talent (even if I couldn't spell).

When you're young, there's a sense of not knowing who you are or what you are. You doubt yourself. There's a lot of pressure from the outside. You worry: Am I enough? Do I act like everyone else? Will I ever be able to learn like everyone else?

I want you to know that you're enough just as you are. What's important is to show up each day despite these doubts. Put one foot in front of other, one word after the other. Sometimes that effort takes more courage than anything else.

—*Jo Ann Yolanda Hernández*